THE KING JUST WENT HOME

J.C. LAYNE

ACKNOWLEDGMENTS

Thanks so much to my readers and friends for your continued support! You all mean the world to me, and I appreciate each of you more than you know! If you enjoy these stories, please tell a friend.

Thanks to the authors and creators We Know the Truth anthology where this story originally appeared. Thanks, especially, to the readers who supported this anthology. This is a silly story spurned from a line in the *Men In Black* movie about one of my most favorite entertainers...who was, incidentally, my very first concert. I hope you enjoy it!

Thanks to Chelly for fitting me in and being so awesome!

Love and hugs to you all! Love rocks!

CHAPTER ONE

"Georgina, hand me them paper towels! I spilt my drank!"

Georgina grumbles as she passes the roll of paper towels across the picnic table, "I sware, woman, you'd be a complete mess without me around to keep you outta trouble!"

Priscilla Mae Jenkins dabs at her breezy, cotton top as she glares at her friend. "I felt one-a them rumbles under foot again. That's what made me take a start and spill that drank."

"You sure it ain't that you've had four a' them thangs since lunch time and it's only two-thirty?" Georgina raises an eyebrow in question.

"Pfft, quit yer bitchin'!" Priscilla rolls her eyes at her friend.

As she continues to mindlessly dab at her top, she looks out into the vastness of the Nevada desert.

Georgina follows her gaze. "What're you starin' at?"

"Oh nothin'…just the…well, the…nothin'."

Georgina huffs out a breath, crossing her arms across her chest. "Well, it's yore brilliant idea that we haaaaaad to come

1

to the damn desert for that stupid Storm Area 51 Facebook thang."

Priscilla stands up straight and plops her hands on her ample hips. "Well, it's better'n sittin' in that damn trailer park watching the damn *Price is Right* and listnin' to Leonore and Fred fightin' all damn night!"

Georgina ponders that statement. "I reckon yore right. So, are we just gonna sit out here in the desert? I mean, what're we gonna do?"

Priscilla gestures, waving her hands wildly. "Look around! It's like a campground already! No tellin' what kinda craziness we'll start seein' come the weekend. And we've got games…you know I can kick yore ass at Jenga!"

Georgina looks around the makeshift RV park to see hundreds of other RVs and camps set up all around them. It's like a festival with all the chattering and excitement.

She asks, "So what's s'posed to happen, agin?"

Priscilla hunkers closer to Georgina, and whispers, "Rumor has it that Area 51 is gonna open some invisible gates and we're all gonna see them aliens they got stored up in there."

Georgina looks around again. "I don't see no gates."

"Did I just say invisible? We ain't s'posed to see them yet. It ain't time! But on the day of the event, the 20th, they say it's gonna get crazy!"

Georgina purses her lips as she shakes her head. It's best just to let her friend ramble at times like these.

CHAPTER TWO

*a*s night falls in the desert, the generators at the RV camps crank up and lights abound, lighting the place like a proper campground. There is even a large spot almost in the center of the mass of camp sites that serves as a park of sorts...where people seem to go to hang out with other people.

Georgina and Priscilla decide they'll go to the open spot for some recon. As much as Georgina fought the idea, Priscilla informed her that they needed to be sociable...and to find out what other people are talking about.

As they carry their folding chairs to the open area, the closer they get, the more chattering they hear. It sounds like more than seems normal. As they walk, they happen onto a group of people in a circle heatedly debating something.

A balding man with a wife beater tank top covering his impressive beer belly is speaking, "I'm tellin' ya, I've seen 'em. They ain't green, they're sort of a shiny blueish color. They do have them big ol' eyes, though."

Another large, burly man spurts, "Oh, bullshit! You ain't see no damn aliens!"

The first man bows up. "I know I have! I was abducted five years ago."

"What'd they do to you, then?" the burly man jests.

Beer belly man replies, "I can't remember. It probably wasn't pleasant, I can tell you that damn much!"

A thin, nervous-looking lady chimes in, "He's right…they are blue…like this iridescent blue. I've seen them, too."

Everyone turns to her as she continues, "They didn't get me, but they got my friend. I seen her bein' taken up in a UFO. I ran and hid in the woods. I thought I'd never see her again, but she showed up at my house the next day. She was outta her gourd, seemed real happy. She ain't been the same ever since. Swears they're livin' among us. She says her friend, Karl, is one of 'em."

Yet another woman, with frizzy auburn hair, adds, "I haven't seem 'em, but I sure want to. They can take me with them. My life sucks so bad, I'd love that opportunity."

Another lady puts her arm around her to comfort her. Georgina and Priscilla are locked arm in arm as they take in all that they are hearing. These people are saying they've seen aliens…actual aliens.

"Holy shit!" Georgina murmurs.

Priscilla and Georgina never make it to sit in their chairs, they just stand the entire time with a death grip on the chairs and each other and listen to all the stories.

After an hour or so, Priscilla squeezes Georgina's arm and mouths, "Let's go."

CHAPTER THREE

*B*ack at their own camp, Priscilla heads straight into the RV and drops into a bench at the small eating area. "What the hell was all that, Georgina?"

She reaches into the nearby cooler and extracts a Lime-a-Rita and pops the top. She takes a long swig then looks over at Georgina expectantly. Georgina hasn't made it past the middle of the RV and is looking a bit shell-shocked.

She finally says, "Gimme one-a them Lime-a-things."

Priscilla passes her a can. Georgina pops the top and takes her own long swig. Then, she states, "I don't know whether to be skeered, excited or to call the men to bring the straight-jackets!"

She swills her Lime-a-Rita again. Priscilla nods. "Yeah, I'm right thar with ya. Them people say they seen them... little blue men."

Georgina sits down across the small table from Priscilla. "I dunno, Priscilla. We might be over our heads with this un!"

Priscilla nods in agreement. Surely, they might be over their heads with this one...

. . .

AFTER TWO MORE LIME-A-RITAS FOR EACH WOMAN, THE ladies fall into their respective beds. Priscilla tries to get comfortable, waiting for the pleasant numbness of the alcohol to take hold of her. When sleep doesn't come, Priscilla tosses and turns instead. Can those people be serious? Have they really seen little blue men?

Suddenly, a bright light streams through the cracks in the RV blinds. Priscilla sits straight up in bed, conking her head on the ceiling before rolling toward the window. Her hand shakes violently as she peeks cautiously out the blinds.

Her eyes widen when she sees a large, gray, disc-shaped aircraft hovering over the open area. There are colored lights circling in series around the craft. The light coming from the bottom of the craft is immense, covering seemingly the entire makeshift RV park with one single beam.

Priscilla's body shakes in fear. Unable to find her voice, she can only stare out the window. Suddenly, a shadow figure seems to float down from the craft, then another, then another. Priscilla's breath is coming in spurts. As the figures disappear among the RVs, Priscilla's eyes roll back in her head and she faints.

CHAPTER FOUR

The next morning, Priscilla is shaken awake. "Wake up, ya crazy loon! Wake up!"

Priscilla startles awake. "Oh, thank tha Lord that we're okay!" she exclaims.

Georgina exclaims, "Okay? Hon, we're great!"

Priscilla looks at her friend with confusion, her brow furrowed. "Great? What ta hell are you talkin' about, woman?"

Grinning, Georgina says, "You were right! Comin' here was a great idea!"

Becoming aggravated, Priscilla snaps, "And why, pray tell, was it such a great idea?"

Georgina looks around before speaking, then moves closer and whispers, "They're comin' back tonight! They say they've gotta surprise for us!"

"Who's gotta surprise for us?"

Georgina whispers again, "The little blue men. They're cute little buggars!"

Priscilla's eyes go wide and she scoots away from Georgina. "H-how do you know that they're cute?"

Georgina states proudly, "'Cause they come and took me up in the spaceship last night!"

Priscilla spurts, "Bullshit! You slept through the entire thang!"

Shaking her head, she argues, "Nah, I didn't sleep through nothin'! I shore did…got took up in tha spaceship! You're the one who was out cold from them Lime-a-thangs!"

Snapping again, Priscilla insists, "I was not out cold from them dranks…I was out cold 'cuz I saw them aliens float down from the ship!"

"You seen 'em, too?"

Priscilla nods, her eyes wide again. "Stop skeerin' me! They didn't take you nowhere!"

Georgina sighs and sits down beside her friend. "They did! Into their spaceship…"

Shaking her head in disbelief, Priscilla snaps, "Well then, Ms. I-went-on-a-spaceship, what'd it look like, huh?"

Georgina scowls and crosses her arms tightly over her chest. "You won't believe me if I told you…"

Priscilla climbs out of her bed, past Georgina to the bench seat at the table. "Try me…"

Georgina takes a deep breath and says, "It looks like a discotheque."

Priscilla stares blankly at her for a few moments, then erupts into laughter. "A discotheque? You're delusional, woman!"

Georgina shakes her head calmly, "Nope…looks just like a discotheque. They really like lights…especially when they bounce off that mirror ball thang."

Priscilla's laughter halts. For a moment, she stares at Georgina. "You're serious, ain't ya?"

Georgina nods. "Yeah, I done told ya. They took me to the spaceship. Three of 'em."

As Priscilla stares at her best friend in confusion,

Georgina begins to ramble, "I told 'em that spaceship lookin' so cool and then the inside lookin' like a set from *Saturday Night Fever* was gold. I told 'em how retro was back in style and that if they'd make a spaceship building and make it a disco nightclub, people would flock to it. I gotta admit, it was purty cool in there. I mean the dranks were a little nasty, but I'm not a big dranker anyway. I leave that up to you. But the cheers was comfy and the movie was good..."

"Movie? And dranks? What did you drank up there?"

She replies, "The movie was *Driving Miss Daisy*..."

Priscilla roars, "*Driving Miss Daisy*? In a discotheque? What ta hell?"

Georgina glares at her. "Yeah, that's what I said, ain't it? What's so damn funny?"

"Only that those things go together like livermush and birthday cake...ain't nobody who'd go to a discotheque wantin' to see no *Driving Miss Daisy*! That's stupid! Hell, why am I even listenin' to ya? I know yore just tellin' me all this to pick on me! I thought you was a better friend than that, Georgina."

Priscilla stands, but before she can take a step, Georgina grabs her arm. "No! Yore gonna listen to me, woman! I ain't lyin' to ya!"

Priscilla remarks sadly, "I think I'm ready to go today. I've 'bout had my fill of aliens."

Georgina replies sharply, "Oh no, we're not goin' anywhere! I know what ta surprise is!"

She begins to giggle like a schoolgirl, irritating Priscilla that much more. Priscilla spits, "What's so damn funny?"

"Yore gonna shit pickles when you see tha surprise!"

Having had enough, Priscilla pounds on the table. She screams, with tears filling her eyes. "Now, that's enough! Stop teasin' me! This ain't funny no more!"

Georgina's smile disappears. "I would never tease ya about The King…"

Priscilla gasps, then squeaks, "Tha real King?"

Georgina chastises herself, "Dammit, dumbass! Give away the surprise, would ya!"

Priscilla plops back down as she squeaks again, "Tha King?"

Georgina nods and smiles. "Yes, Elvis Presley. Yore idol!"

Georgina sits down across from Priscilla at the tiny eating table. "I didn't wanna spoil the surprise fer ya. I knowed you was gonna freak out."

Finally, able to string a sentence together, Priscilla asks, "Wh-what does Elvis hafta do with this?"

Georgina replies, "Well, The King is gonna perform here tonight. He ain't really dead, y'know. He just went home. That wasn't no lie they said in that *Men in Black* movie!"

Priscilla spits, "Are you tryin' to tell me Elvis Presley is an alien?"

Georgina grins. "Anyone with that much talent can't be from this here planet!"

Priscilla stands and bows up. Hands on her hips and red-faced, she yells, "Take it back! Take it back right now, Georgina Louise Parker!"

Georgina stares at her with confusion, as she straightens her shoulders. "I won't do it! I seen him…looks just like he did at the *Aloha from Hawaii* special!"

Priscilla shrieks, "Liar! He ain't no alien!"

Getting angry now, Georgina replies, "I reckon you'll see…" and turns and saunters out of the RV.

CHAPTER FIVE

*L*ater that day, after a day of the silent treatment and a lot of playing of the "American Trilogy" by none-other-than-The-King, himself, Priscilla finally says, "Awright, Georgina. Tell me what exactly happened last night..."

Georgina sighs, but recaps being taken up into the space-ship, sitting in the discotheque-decored room with the cute little blue men. She elaborates on the drinks they gave her... something called Cosmic Stress with some sort of vodka-like liquor and this fruit juice like she'd never tasted before. The little blue guys seemed to love it and quite a few got snock-ered before she was escorted back to her RV by the three who picked her up. But, to her, it tasted like what motor oil should taste like, if she drank it on the regular. While she was there, she had her drinks, watched the little blue men party and dance to disco music, watched *Driving Miss Daisy*, played monopoly, and met the one and only Elvis Presley.

Priscilla listens intently, trying not to react when Georgina says something she doesn't believe...which is pretty much the entire story. She finally asks, "So, they didn't try to anal probe you or put any kind of bugs on you while you was thar or nothin'?"

Georgina shakes her head. "Nope, nothin' like that. They just like humans and hangin' out with us."

Priscilla asks, "Were there other humans there?"

"Oh yeah. The guy with the wife beater shirt was there. They knew him by name, so I reckon he was tellin' the truth. Ha! That big noisy guy can apologize to him, I reckon!"

Priscilla's brow furrows. "But I thought he said they was awful little men."

"No, that was that woman, who didn't meet 'em but seen 'em take her friend. Said her friend wasn't never the same, 'member?"

Priscilla agrees, "Oh yeah. "

Georgina nods. "I ain't lying to ya, Pris. I promise. I ain't believin' it happened myself!"

It's Priscilla's turn to nod. "It's just…unbelievable."

Georgina nods again. "It shore is."

CHAPTER SIX

a couple of hours later, when the sun has set and the RV park is lit with lights of all kinds, Georgina looks at her watch, "We'd better get ready. We want a good seat for The King!"

Priscilla reckons she should look fabulous just in case Georgina isn't completely off her rocker. If she's having a chance to see The King, she's gonna look damn good for it!

Priscilla tells Georgina, "I've gotta get gorgeous. Might take a few minutes."

"I figured you would," laughs Georgina as she leaves the RV and shuts the door behind her.

Forty-five minutes later, Priscilla Mae Jenkins emerges from the RV dressed to the nines. Her bottle red hair is teased into a large bouffant hairdo. Her face is covered with full makeup from the blue eyeshadow to the thick black eyeliner, to the princess pink rouge covering her cheeks to the regal red lipstick on her full lips. She wears leggings adorned with sequins placed among the cheetah-print fabric. Her black top is tight and pulled down over her hips with a belt over it accentuating her now not-so-small waist. The outfit is completed by four-inch hot pink wedge sandals and matching three-inch hot pink wooden circle earrings.

Georgina looks up from her chair where she has been reading the latest *National Enquirer*. When Georgina sees her, she laughs. "Hoo-weee! You mean business tonight, don'tcha, girl? You sorta look like Peg Bundy!"

Priscilla harrumphs. "Pfft! Peg Bundy ain't got nothin' on me! If there's a chance to see The King, I'm gonna look my absolute best. I do have tha same name as his ex-wife, y'know?"

"That you do, girl," Georgina says as she folds up her magazine and stands. She hands Priscilla a folding chair, then folds up her own. "Come on, let's go get us a good spot."

As Georgina leads the way, Priscilla teeters behind her, her wedge sandals sinking into the sand. Bad fashion move in the dessert, Priscilla thinks.

As she teeters along, Priscilla asks, "How do you know where to go?"

Georgina remarks, "They told me where to be."

Suddenly, Georgina stops walking and sets her chair down. Priscilla follows suit. It's an odd place to set the chairs, right in the middle of where people are standing, but Priscilla has to trust her BFF. Looking around, she notices several other people sitting in chairs in the middle of the people milling about, too. One of the people is the man in the wife beater and his companion. He holds up his can of Coors Light in a toast gesture. Georgina waves back. She whispers, "His name is Lester. Like I said, they knowed him by name. He must really be a frequent flyer…"

She glances at her watch then murmurs, "It's almost time. Get ready, girl!"

On cue, an all-consuming light comes down on them

from the sky. It's so bright against the pale sand that Priscilla has to cover her eyes. Georgina just claps wildly.

An odd whirring sound can be heard but Priscilla can't see anything due to the brightness of the light, but she tries to look around anyway. She yells, "Georgina, I can't see a damn thang!"

"Hang on, girl! He's almost down!"

Priscilla hears a thud and the light simultaneously goes out. The lights around the compound seem to have been extinguished by the bright light.

At this moment, they're all sitting in the pitch dark. Some people are rushing around screaming, some frozen in their tracks. Georgina and Priscilla sit silently in their folding chairs, completely engulfed in the dark, waiting...waiting expectantly for Elvis Presley.

Suddenly, a stage looking very much like a discotheque roars to life. Every instrument from a normal rock band and an entire brass/woodwind section is represented, played, of course, by little blue men with big, orbed eyes.

Priscilla sits with her mouth open, seeming to take it all in. The band begins to play "2001: A Space Odyssey" which is the entrance song for none other than Elvis Presley.

Priscilla gasps and grabs Georgina's arm in a tight grasp. She murmurs, "It's him...it's really him...omigosh, omigosh..."

In a split second, a little blue man dressed in a replica of Elvis's *Aloha from Hawaii* jumpsuit rushes onto stage. The little blue man has an Elvis wig and large gold sunglasses to complete his get up.

Priscilla's heart drops to her feet. She'd been fooled by her best friend. She bends at her waist and drops her face into her hands and begins to cry. The crowd around her continues to scream and cheer for the little blue fake Elvis.

The intro is over and the musicians begin to play "Suspicious Minds." A voice breaks through the music...that voice...so pristine, so smooth, so perfect. She'd know it anywhere.

Priscilla lifts her head to look at the stage. There he is...in all his glory...Elvis Presley. Her idol. He's as handsome as ever, his voice as close to perfection as one can get. He sings, playing to the crowd as he covers the stage moving lithely from one end to the other.

There he is, only thirty feet from her. The next song begins. It is "Love Me Tender." Every woman in the crowd rushes to the stage, including Priscilla and Georgina, to await a scarf, a serenade and a kiss on the cheek.

As Elvis moves from the opposite side of the stage, he seems to make a bee-line for Priscilla. He crouches right in front of her, his handsome face only inches from her. As he drapes a scarf around her neck, he whispers, "It's good to see you again, Priscilla." She gasps, studying his face, burning it into her mind for the future. He winks, kisses her on the cheek and is off to make another woman happy.

Priscilla's hand covers her cheek as she slowly returns to her seat. She's seemingly in a trance as she turns back to the stage. Georgina rushes back to her, her own scarf around her neck.

She grins broadly. "I told ya..."

Priscilla nods detachedly, "You shore did. How did...I mean...where has...what's happening?"

Georgina laughs as the band begins to play "Promised Land."

Georgina replies, "Well, let's see here. We've learned that aliens are real, that they're cute little blue men, that they like discos and disco music, they have strange taste in movies, and that Area 51 is whar The King, who is also an alien and alive, likes to play ta believers. I'd say our trip ta Area 51 has been worth tha drive.

Priscilla nods. "I guess they was right. The King really did just go home."

ABOUT THE AUTHOR

J.C. Layne is an avid music fan, reader and geek. J.C. combines her passion and knowledge of music with her love of fiction in her novels. By day, J.C. holds a technical job in a large company. Writing is the outlet that balances out her techie left-side brain and creative right-side brain...and hopefully keeps her sane.

J.C. started out writing rock star romance but has expanded into multiple genres. She has been part of contemporary and erotic anthologies and is part of the paranormal Black Hollow series with five other fabulous authors and friends.

J.C. lives in Charlotte, NC with her three fur babies. She is a die-hard Carolina Panthers and South Carolina Gamecocks fan and a writer for various music media outlets.

To learn more about J.C. please visit her online at www.authorjclayne.com.

You can also find her on Facebook at www.facebook.com/authorjclayne

ALSO BY J.C. LAYNE

Made in the USA
Columbia, SC
22 May 2023

16462330R10015